The year is 1144 and the world's last dragon has returned. The evil Lord Manning plans to use that dragon to rule the kingdom. According to prophecy, only one person can stop him. And that one person is a 16-year-old boy.

BOOK 1: *The Last Dragon* Jacob, Orson and Lia must rescue the only egg of the world's last dragon.

BOOK 2: *A Hero's Worth* While the young dragon grows, Lia may be forced to marry Lord Manning.

BOOK 3: *Draco's Fire* The fully grown dragon helps Jacob fulfill the prophecy — and rescue his kingdom.

The DRAGON SPEAKER Series

A Hero's Worth

D.M. OUELLET

LIBRARY AND ARCHIVES CANADA CATALOGUING IN PUBLICATION

Ouellet, Debbie
  A hero's worth / D.A. Ouellet.

(HIP fantasy)
(Dragon speaker ; 2)
ISBN 978-1-897039-47-2

I. Title. II. Series: HIP fantasy III. Series: Dragon speaker ; 2

PS8629.U33H47 2009   jC813'.6   C2009-903744-0

General editor: Paul Kropp
Text design: Laura Brady
Illustrations drawn by: Charlie Hnatiuk
Cover design: Robert Corrigan

2 3 4 5 6   09 10 11 12 13

Printed and bound in Canada

High Interest Publishing acknowledges the financial support of the
Government of Canada through the Book Publishing Industry
Development Program (BPIDP) for our publishing activities.

CONTENTS

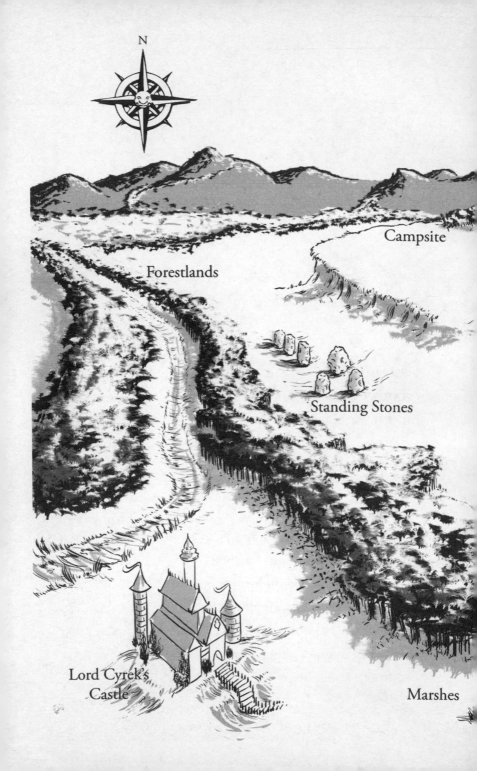

Claw Mountain

Mound Meadow

Farmlands

Lord Manning's Castle

Pine Abbey

Market Town

Great Forest

Village of Maldon

To my own heroes: Ray, Alex and Sarah

Prologue

These are dark times. The people suffer under the iron fist of Lord Manning. The heroes of the past are dead. The dragons of old have been killed. There seems to be no chance of rescue for the kingdom.

But there is a prophecy.

When a dragon born of Draco's fire
once more shall walk this earth,
the Chosen One must pay the cost
to test a hero's worth.

Lord Manning believes the prophecy. He fears a dragon that could destroy him. He fears the birds, the Dragon's cousins. He fears the young people who dare to speak the dragon's name.

But where there is evil, there is also hope. Far from the eyes of Lord Manning and his wizard hides the Chosen One. He is only a boy with a twisted leg. But in his arms he holds the hope of his people.

It is young.

It is helpless.

It is the last dragon.

CHAPTER ONE | Visitors in the Night

The night was cold. Jacob gathered twigs, then struck a flint until a spark flared. The twigs lit and a small fire glowed. Fire was risky here. Someone might see it. But the bundle in Jacob's arms was shivering. The dragon — the last fire dragon — was cold and hungry.

"Here, try this." Lia handed Jacob some flesh she'd skinned from a rabbit. "This baby sure makes a lot of noise when he's hungry."

Jacob put the meat to the dragon's mouth. *Eat this.* Jacob sent his thoughts to the dragon. *And please be quiet. We're supposed to be hiding.*

The dragon sounded like a calf, only the tone was deeper. It was a throaty bellow that one day would grow into a roar.

Hungry! the dragon answered. But only Jacob could hear its thoughts.

While the baby dragon ate, Jacob watched the fire. The flames made shadows on Lia's pale face. The head scarf she always wore was tied tight around her golden-brown hair. Jacob wondered about this girl, this dragon healer. She never talked about herself. She never talked of her family, her village, her life.

Lia had only a light shawl around her shoulders. Didn't she feel the cold? Even wearing his deer-skin pelt, Jacob felt his teeth chattered. But this girl didn't seem to need the fire's warmth.

When the dragon stopped eating, there was silence. The small dragon nuzzled Jacob's arm and slept. If the prophecy was right, this dragon would one day save their people. But how? Right now, all it did was eat and sleep.

Nearby, a twig snapped. Lia's eyes widened. She put her finger to her lips and drew her knife. Jacob reached for his bow. He covered the dragon with a blanket.

Before the stranger could step into their campsite, Lia had jumped to her feet.

"Relax, girl," the stranger said. "I only want to warm my bones at your fire."

The man was older than dirt. White tufts of hair stuck out from his hooded cloak. He leaned his wrinkled body on a walking staff.

"State your business and be quick about it," Jacob ordered. He had his bow ready. The arrow was aimed at the old man's chest.

Suddenly, the old man raised his staff and struck. In a flurry of moves, Lia's knife was knocked to the ground. Then Jacob's bow flew from his fingers. And finally, with a flick of his staff, the old man forced Jacob to the ground.

But the old man was smiling. "It seems your parents haven't taught you proper respect for your elders. Let this be your first lesson," the old man said. As quickly as he'd held them down, he let Jacob and Lia go. "I have no quarrel with children."

Jacob's temper sparked. "I am sixteen years old!"

"I do apologize," the old man said with a nod. "I have no quarrel with young men . . . or women." He smiled, then moved closer to the fire. As he warmed his hands, he pulled the hood back from his head. "Have you forgotten me so quickly?"

"Aldous?" Jacob asked. He remembered Lord

Manning's dungeon. It was Aldous who helped him escape. All that felt like a lifetime ago. Still, he'd repaid his debt to the old man. To Jacob's mind, they were even. Why had Aldous turned up now? Why was he here when they were protecting the dragon?

Jacob hardened his stare. "What do you want?"

"I've been following you." Aldous helped himself to some rabbit they'd skinned and cooked. "And I'm hungry." He pulled a flask of wine from the pocket of his cloak. Soon he had washed down the rabbit.

"Following us? Why?" Jacob kept his voice firm.

"I'm here to warn you. Lord Manning has offered ten gold pieces to the man who brings him your head. He's offered fifty gold pieces for the head of the little dragon you're hiding under that blanket."

Jacob gulped. He tucked the blanket tighter around the dragon. Slowly, he moved to where his bow had fallen. "How do I know you're not here to claim the reward?"

Jacob dove for his bow. Lia retrieved her knife. Both stood ready to protect the sleeping dragon.

"Didn't we just do this?" Aldous sighed. Crack! Aldous knocked Jacob's bow from his hands with the butt of his staff. He was about to hit Lia's knife, but the dragon stirred in its blanket.

A small bellow echoed in the air. Before Jacob could stop it, the dragon shook off his blanket. As if he'd sensed their need, the young dragon charged at Aldous. His tiny wings were spread. His ears lay flat against his small square head. He snapped and snarled at the old man.

Aldous fell to his knees. He slowly placed his staff on the ground. Then he spread his hands out, palms up. "Come, little one. You've nothing to fear from me."

The dragon attempted a growl. It backed away from Aldous until it bumped against Jacob's bad leg.

Jacob winced. His leg still hurt from all that had happened. Jacob kept the pain to himself, as he always did, but the pain was real.

Still, the dragon stayed in front of Jacob. The baby was trying to protect him.

Aldous made a steeple of his hands, then pressed them to his lips. "Would I have told you about the price on your heads if I meant to collect it? I'm only here to help."

"Help? How do you plan to do that?" Jacob challenged.

"For one thing, I'll teach you to hide better." Aldous folded his arms in front of him. "If I can find you, so can Kain and his men."

"Why would you do that?" Lia asked. "Why would you risk your own neck for us … or the dragon?"

"Because this is the dragon of the prophecy," Aldous explained. "Nothing matters more to me than seeing this little one fulfill that prophecy."

Aldous reached his hand out to the growling dragon. It sniffed him once, then bellowed softly. Then it bumped its nose against the old man's hand.

Friend, the dragon sent to Jacob.

"It looks like the dragon trusts you," Jacob told the old man.

Aldous patted the dragon's head. "I pledge my staff and my life to your service, little one. No harm will come to you as long as I draw breath."

Jacob looked into his eyes and knew the old man spoke the truth. Jacob motioned for Lia to put down her knife.

"What other news do you bring?" Lia asked.

Aldous took another drink from his wine flask. "Only that the villagers are talking about the Dragon Speaker."

"What are they saying?"

"That he's six feet tall. Big muscles. A giant of a man, or so they say." Aldous winked at Jacob.

Lia laughed and Jacob glared at her. She lowered her head to cover her face in her hair. He could still see her shoulders shaking.

~

The three of them talked well into the night. By midnight, Lia was curled up like a cat, sleeping. The old man had drunk himself to sleep. But Jacob was awake.

As the fire died, Jacob looked up into the clear night sky. Draco, the dragon of the stars, was in the north. *They say the souls of all dragons are in those stars*, Jacob thought. Then he sent the thought as he patted the young dragon's head. *That's what I'll call you. Draco. Do you like that name?*

A good name. The dragon nuzzled Jacob's hand with its nose.

Draco it is, then.

As Jacob stared into the heavens, a star fell. Unlike other stars Jacob had seen, this one had a ghostly green glow. *A bad omen*, Jacob thought. A pin prick of fear raced down Jacob's spine just as he heard the sound of a horse's hooves.

In no time, Jacob was on his feet, his bow and arrow aimed at the sound. The bushes shook and Jacob almost loosed an arrow before he heard the voice.

"Whoa," Orson called out. "It's me."

Orson pushed his way into the clearing, then up to the fire. "Jacob, I think you should come to the village."

"What? Has something else happened?" Fear snaked around Jacob's heart. "Has Kain attacked again?"

"No, nothing like that. But there is a funeral tomorrow … for your father. We know that Lord Manning's soldiers will be watching, but still, you should be there. Or at least be close."

Jacob sighed. "I'll go. I'm the last of the family. It's my duty."

"And I'll go with you," Orson replied, "just to make sure you don't get caught."

CHAPTER TWO | Kain Will Pay

Jacob and Orson reached the village just after dawn. Even from outside the walls, they could see wood for the funeral pyre. Some of the villagers were laying the wood. The body of Jacob's father lay on a folded blanket nearby.

"I should go," Jacob said. "I should say something. I should offer a prayer."

"No, you should stay right here," Orson told him. "Look over at those two huts. Can't you see the soldiers inside? They're just waiting for you."

"But still. . . ."

"And if they get you, Jacob, then they'll find all of us. And Draco, too." Orson waited for his words to sink in. "You can say your prayer from here."

Jacob sighed. His friend was right, of course. There was no point charging into the village. He'd be captured and taken right to Lord Manning. That's what Manning and Kain were counting on. They expected Jacob to be a fool.

So Jacob and Orson stayed outside the village, hidden from sight. They could hear the sound of drumming. Then a gong sounded three times. Slowly the villagers gathered. In two and threes, alone and in families, they stood around the funeral pyre.

The village priest appeared. He chanted a few words, while others lifted the body onto the pyre. There was a moment of silence. Then the priest brought a burning torch to the dried leaves under the pyre. The pyre went up in flames.

At first, Jacob could not shed a tear. But as the fire grew, Jacob knew that he'd never see his father again. And he broke down.

"It's all right," Orson said, patting him on the shoulder. "His death wasn't your fault. You did the best you could."

"It's not that," Jacob replied. "It's just ... well, he's my father."

That was the simple truth. Jacob's father had been a good man, at least until his wife and elder son were killed. He'd worked hard for his family. He'd been true to King Harold. And his reward had been death for his family, and then himself.

Surely these were the darkest of times.

"Come, my friend," Orson said. "Let's get back to the others."

Orson guided Jacob away. Orson kept looking around for soldiers who might be waiting for them. Jacob was lost in his own thoughts. At first, he was just sad. Then the sadness turned to anger. At last, the anger turned into a vow.

Kain would pay for his father's death.

~

It was early the next day when Jacob rode into the hidden campsite. The long ride took its toll on his leg. He limped to where they'd stored their food and clothing.

"Jacob?" Lia put her hand on his shoulder.

Jacob brushed it away. He didn't want her pity. "I only came back to get supplies."

"What are you going to do?"

"What do you think? Kain killed my father!" Jacob stuffed bread and cheese into a sack. He slung his bow over his shoulder.

"No, Jacob!" Lia forced him to look at her. "Can't you see? This is what Kain wants. He's using your father to get to you, and using you to get to the dragon."

Orson was practicing with his sword nearby. When he heard the story, he agreed with Lia. "She's right, Jacob. Kain's playing with you. He wants you to come after him."

Jacob glared at his friends. "Then he won't be disappointed."

As he stomped away, Jacob's leg buckled. He fell with a thud. Sack, bow and arrows scattered on the ground. White hot pain shot through him.

When Lia came to help, he pushed away her hands. Then he struggled to his knees. When Jacob tried to stand, a staff touched the small of his back. The pressure sent him sprawling again.

"I'd say your friends offer good advice," Aldous told him. The old man removed his staff and kneeled beside Jacob.

"This doesn't concern you, old man," Jacob snapped.

Aldous ignored him. "Let me look at your leg. I know about these things." Aldous put his finger in the tear in

Jacob's sock, then ripped. Beneath the sock were many ugly, twisted scars.

Jacob covered them with his hands. He hated when anyone saw them, but Aldous brushed Jacob's hand aside. He nodded to Lia and the two healers went to work.

Healing is half magic, half wisdom. Aldous put some herbs on Jacob's leg. Lia held her hands over his leg and chanted. In time, the swelling in Jacob's leg went back to normal. His leg was still scarred, still ugly, but it no longer hurt. Aldous wrapped it tight in a brace made of leather strips. This time, when Jacob stood, his leg was steady.

The fire of Jacob's anger had gone down, but not his resolve. "This doesn't change anything. I'm still going," he told them.

Orson and Lia traded glances.

Orson picked up his sword and sheathed it. "Not without me, you aren't."

Lia tucked her blade into her belt. "Same goes for me."

"I don't deserve friends like you," Jacob told them. "But who is going to look after Draco?"

The three of them looked at Aldous. The old man nodded and smiled. "It will be an honor," he told them.

Saying goodbye to Draco was hard. Jacob looked into the dragon's golden eyes. He focused his thoughts. *I'll be back in a few days. I promise*, he sent.

Jacob! Draco bellowed.

Aldous will watch over you. Jacob mounted his horse. *You can trust him.*

Aldous placed his hand on Draco's leathery head. The baby dragon made a cooing sound. But long after Jacob rode away, Draco's cries echoed in Jacob's head. *Jacob! Don't go!*

CHAPTER THREE | Danger. Turn Back!

Jacob, Orson and Lia rode hard for five hours, tracing and retracing their steps.

"That should do it," Jacob told the others. "No one can track us back to the campsite now."

After another hour, Jacob motioned them to stop at a stream. "Let the horses rest and drink."

Orson used the chance to practice more with his sword. Thrust. Slice. Withdraw. Jacob envied how light his friend was on his feet. His sword-fighting was like a dance.

"Don't you ever get tired of that?" Jacob asked.

"I'm never going to be a knight if I'm not good with a sword." Orson danced around some more. "The festival isn't far away, you know. It's my big chance."

Orson had always had one dream. He wanted to compete at the Samain Festival. If Orson could win in swordplay, they'd let him try out to become a knight.

Lia stood beside Jacob. She had little interest in Orson's workout. "When you get to the castle, how will you find Kain?" she asked.

"I'm going to ask for help," Jacob told her. At Lia's puzzled look, he added, "There is one bonus to being a dragon speaker."

All birds were distant cousins of dragons, and Jacob could speak to them too. Jacob called to the birds as he stood with Lia. Like musical notes, his thoughts flew from treetop to field. From field to hillside. From hillside to stream. Each bird passed on the question that Jacob formed in his mind. *Cousins. Where is Kain?* Jacob waited until the answer came back to him. *Among the standing stones. Where the valley and Forestlands meet.*

But there were other words that came with them. *Danger. Turn back.* Jacob brushed those words from his mind. He told Orson and Lia to gather their things. It was time.

The three friends rode until they came to the path

leading into the valley. Huge standing stones formed a circle in its center. To the north and east were rugged cliffs. To the west were the Forestlands. If there were problems, this place would be a nightmare. The cliffs would block any escape. The Forestlands were claimed by the Elven Lord. No human ever dared go in there.

"I don't like this." Orson drew his sword.

Lia gripped her small blade. "We should go back."

Jacob looked at the valley below. Kain could be hiding anywhere. The path they rode was the only clear way in. If they were going to find Kain, this was their one chance. But Jacob remembered the thoughts of the birds. *Danger. Turn back.* He was ready to do just that when he heard a voice.

"Took your time getting here, boy."

Jacob froze. Lia's horse rose up on its hooves. Orson pulled out his sword.

Kain stepped out into the clearing between the huge stones. His black cloak snapped in the wind. The teeth in his hair clicked. He spread his arms wide, daring Jacob to strike. "What are you waiting for?" When Jacob didn't answer, Kain threw back his head and laughed. "Just as I thought. No backbone. You're just like your father."

Blood rushed up Jacob's spine. He raised his fist and let out a cry of anger. The ground shook with the sound of hooves as Jacob raced into the valley. Orson and Lia followed behind him.

Jacob was soon within range of the wizard. He drew his bow and aimed. His arrow sliced through the air.

Kain swatted it away like a man might swat a fly. "Is that all, boy?" Kain took off his cloak and threw it to the ground. "Let's do this like men, shall we? Just you and me. No magic."

"Don't listen to him, Jacob," Orson urged his friend. "You can't trust him."

But Jacob was past listening. He was past thinking. All he could do was feel. White hot anger burned through him as he urged his horse forward. They entered the clearing where Kain waited.

Lia trailed behind. "I've a bad feeling. We should go back."

Jacob wasn't listening. He dismounted and walked forward. The brace on his leg pinched, but it held his weight. He drew his bow and shot again.

The arrow shot true, headed right for Kain's throat. But Kain moved just as it was about to strike.

"Did you really think I'd make it that easy, boy?" Kain took a carved white whistle from his pocket and blew it. Suddenly, men poured from behind the stones like ants from an anthill.

Jacob's arrows flew at the men, fast and furious. Orson joined his friend. He thrust and sliced with his sword. Lia spun with knife in hand, cutting anyone within arm's reach. But for every man they cut down, two more came.

"If you've got any more bright ideas, now's the time." Orson shouted to Jacob.

"I'm still thinking," Jacob shouted back, but he was running out of arrows.

Then a lance whizzed through the air. Orson ducked, but Lia cried out as it sliced her shoulder.

"Lia!" Jacob cried, turning toward her.

That was a mistake. Jacob lost focus on the battle. It was only for a moment, but that was long enough for Kain to sneak up from behind. He grabbed Jacob by the throat and shoved him against a standing stone.

Orson tried to reach his friend, but Kain's men made a wall to keep them apart.

Kain forced Jacob's jaws apart. He ran a blackened thumb across Jacob's open mouth. "Good strong teeth, boy."

Jacob struggled, but couldn't get free.

"You see this, boy?" Kain pointed to a tooth tied into one of his braids. "We'll make it a family, shall we? I'm going to add one of yours to my hair. It will be much more of a prize than your father's."

How stupid could I be? Jacob thought. *This is all my fault.*

Kain's breath was foul against Jacob's cheek. "Hear this well, boy. The prophecy will never be. Your dragon will never live to see it through."

Jacob closed his mind to Kain's voice. He reached deep into himself. *Cousins!* he sent the thought. Jacob pictured sharp claws. Hooked beaks. He pictured an attack that might just save them.

Suddenly, day was made night. The sky filled with eerie shrieks. A thousand wings covered the sun. Like a great soaring cloud they attacked. Eagles, hawks, owls — they fought as one great flying army.

A sparrowhawk swooped. She dug her claws into Kain's skull. *Run!* she sent to Jacob.

Jacob ducked from Kain's grasp. His heart pounded. His ears rang. And he ran, faster than he'd ever run before.

"We've got to get out of here!" he called to Orson and Lia.

Eagles and hawks still swooped and struck. Swooped and struck. They bought enough time for Jacob to reach his horse. The brace on his leg bit into his flesh as he mounted, but he ignored the pain. He reached down and helped Lia onto her horse. Her arm was bleeding badly now.

Once he saw that Orson had mounted his horse, Jacob took Lia's horse by the reins. "Hold on!" he called to her.

"Where are we going?" Orson cried.

"Into the Forestlands," Jacob called back.

"No!" Lia tried to pull the reins from Jacob's hand. "We can't go in there."

Jacob held the reins tightly. "We don't have any choice."

As they entered the forest, Jacob braved one look back. Eagles, hawks and owls lay slaughtered. Hundreds of birds lay in a sea of feathers and blood. Jacob could feel the life leave them.

What had he done? And what could they do now?

CHAPTER FOUR | Elves!

They made camp an hour's trek into the forest. Lia sat silently while Jacob bandaged her arm. The bleeding had stopped, but still she was in pain.

Jacob was worried about her. Lia had fought beside him before, but she had never acted so strangely. So afraid. Lia's eyes were wild. She kept looking over her shoulder into the trees. It was as if she was afraid of the trees themselves.

Evening came and Orson snored in his sleep. Jacob tended the fire while Lia stared into the night.

"What's wrong, Lia?"

Lia fixed her head scarf. "Nothing."

"I'm sorry. . . ." Jacob searched for words.

"What?"

"I'm sorry for all … this."

"Don't feel sorry, Jacob," Lia told him. "I understand why you went after Kain. He killed your entire family."

"Wouldn't you have done the same?"

Lia avoided his eyes. "My father and I don't … speak."

"Why? What happened?"

Lia covered a yawn. "I'm tired. It's time to get some sleep." She pulled a blanket over her and turned her back to Jacob and his questions.

When morning came, Jacob's body ached. He had slept poorly. Through the night, emotions boiled in his blood. He was angry with Kain for all he'd done. He was angry with himself for putting his friends at risk. And he was full of regret for the lives lost so far.

How many more would die in Jacob's quest? And would their deaths be worth it?

Jacob sat by the stream, deep in thought. He was skipping stones across the water when Lia came to wash up.

"Morning," she mumbled.

Lia took a cloth and dipped it into the frigid water, then scrubbed her face.

Jacob watched the water trickle down her neck. He noticed the curve of her pale cheek. He saw a few curls under the head scarf. Did she ever take off that scarf? He imagined her without it, her hair loose in the wind. He wondered how her hair would feel in his hands.

Stop it! Jacob told himself. He was flushed and embarrassed. "This isn't a lady's parlour," he said, hiding his feelings. "Hurry up. We need to break camp."

The silence was thick between Jacob and Lia when they returned to the campsite.

Orson was packing away their pots and food. "Took you two long enough," he said, staring at them. "I'm almost done. Or was that the pla . . . ?" Orson's eyes narrowed. He creased his brow, then tilted his head. In a flash, Orson had his sword drawn.

Jacob felt it too. There were eyes watching them. He reached for his bow.

Suddenly, men came out from the trees. There were half a dozen tall, pale men with bows and spears. They had long flowing hair and smooth faces. Their ears came to a sharp point.

Elves!

Jacob let all his arrows fly. Orson charged with his sword. Lia twirled and kicked, her knife flashing in the sun. Soon the elves retreated into the woods.

"Well, that was easy." Orson swung his sword blade in a circle.

Jacob lowered his bow and arrows. "It's all right, Lia," Jacob said. He touched her shoulder as a signal to lower her weapon.

"No," she whispered. "It's not all right."

Suddenly the forest echoed with a terrible sound. It was the sound of hundreds of spears beating the ground. The pounding sounded like thunder. Then a double line of Elven guards marched through the trees.

Jacob raised his bow. Orson readied his sword. But both knew they had no chance against so many elves.

"Lia," Jacob urged. "Come closer."

Lia stayed glued to her spot.

The lines of guards separated. Suddenly an old, wrinkled elf walked through the middle. The two lines of guards bowed low. The old elf had white hair that reached his waist. He wore a robe of leaves with feathers and twigs woven into it. A crown sat on his head, its golden leaves formed into the shape of twisted vines.

"It's Cyrek! The Elven Lord," Orson whispered.

The thumping of spears on the ground was deafening. The old elf raised his hand.

Silence.

Jacob and Orson placed themselves on either side of Lia. "Wait for my signal," Jacob whispered. "If we move fast. . . ."

But Jacob had no time to explain his plan. Lia had already started walking forward. She threw her blade to the ground and kneeled down before the Elven lord.

The old elf reached his hand down to Lia's chin, then raised her face to look at his.

"How long did you think you could hide from me, little one?"

CHAPTER FIVE | Lia's Choice

Jacob tried to help Lia. He was almost at her side when the point of a guard's spear touched his neck. "Kneel before Lord Cyrek," the guard growled.

Lia turned her head in Jacob's direction, but her eyes were full of tears.

Why didn't she fight? Jacob wondered.

Cyrek grabbed Lia roughly by the shoulder, forcing her to stand. "Do you find shame in what you are, Lia?"

Lia said nothing.

"Why do you hide it? Why do you hide your real

self?" With a flick of his wrist, Cyrek ripped the scarf from Lia's head. "This is what you are!"

Her ears! This time, the guard didn't have to force Jacob to kneel. He fell dumbly to the ground. Jacob's eyes were wide. His jaw swung open like a hinged door. Lia had pointed ears. This girl, this girl who had spent so many days with them, was an elf!

Lia lifted her chin. She pulled the head scarf from Cyrek's fingers. Her hands shook as she tied it once morearound her head. "No, Father, this is what I am."

For a moment, Cyrek looked like he might strike her. The old elf clenched and unclenched his jaw. The silence between them grew as sharp as the edge of a knife.

"So be it." Cyrek spat out the words. "Guards, escort my daughter back to the castle." He pointed to Jacob and Orson. "See that these two are put in chains."

"Father, no!" Lia pleaded. But Cyrek had already turned his back and strode into the woods.

~

Morning came. Jacob and Orson had spent two days in chains. The dirt floor beneath them was damp and cold. The stone walls around them stank of death. Jacob's leg

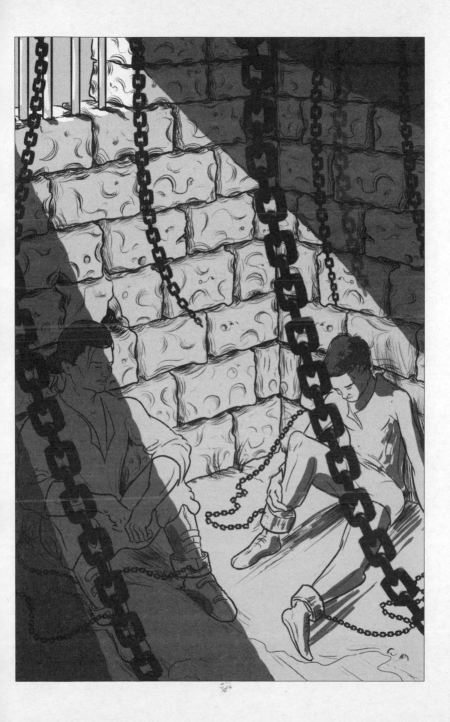

irons bit into his flesh, like a wolf chewing on bone. Orson had a bracelet of purple welts on each wrist. They'd had no food or water since being captured.

"Orson?" Jacob shook his friend's shoulder. "Are you all right?"

Orson coughed and forced a smile. "Other than being chained to a stone wall and hungry enough to eat my boots, I'm fine. Just great."

Jacob couldn't even smile.

Jacob could hear the master jailor, a small fat troll, as he stomped through the halls outside. A whip cracked and someone cried out in pain. Jacob flinched with each strike. Then he heard a heavy axe being lifted from the wall. There was a cry of terror. A whoosh and a thwack. Then silence.

Jacob touched his neck and gulped. Somehow they had to find a way out of here. And fast.

As morning turned to midday, Jacob dozed. He was startled awake by the sound of the master jailor grinding his axe. He wondered if, this time, the axe was for him or Orson.

Far off, a heavy door opened and closed. Footsteps hurried down the rough stone stairs. The troll poked his head through the small opening in the cell door.

"You got company," he said through broken teeth.

The cell door groaned open. A shaft of light cut into the darkness. For a moment, Jacob was blinded. When his vision cleared, he couldn't believe his eyes.

Lia stood before him. But not the Lia he remembered from the riverbank. Not the Lia who wore a simple tunic and a head scarf. The Lia at his cell door was a princess. She wore a green silk gown that sparkled like dew on a leaf. Her golden hair hung to the back of her knees. There were jewels tucked into her curls.

Lia stood with her hands clasped tightly together. Her father, Cyrek, towered behind her.

Two guards entered. They put the points of their spears at the necks of Jacob and Orson. The message was clear. They were to keep their mouths shut.

"You see, daughter, I've kept my word. Your friends are unharmed." Cyrek took Lia's arm and brought her where Jacob and Orson sat chained to the wall.

The sound of the troll grinding his axe hummed in the background.

"What are you going to do with them?" Lia avoided Jacob's eyes. She looked at the floor as she spoke.

"That depends entirely on you, my dear." Cyrek placed his hand beneath Lia's chin. He forced her to look at him.

"What do you want?" Lia's eyes glared into his.

"A bargain." The Elven lord crossed his arms like battle swords. "Lord Manning makes no secret that he finds you attractive." He raised a hand to silence Lia when she protested. "And it's high time you took a husband. Manning has title and lands. Did you really think I'd accept anything less than a lord for my only daughter?"

"Manning is an evil man, Father. The humans suffer under his rule."

"I wouldn't waste my spit on a human," Cyrek growled. "Let them kill each other off for all I care. Just so long as our people are kept out of it."

"But father, I don't love him," Lia said in a whisper.

"Love!" Cyrek threw back his head and laughed. "Love has nothing to do with this. I'm talking about land and power. I've fought hard and long to acquire my claim to the Forestlands. In exchange for your hand in marriage, Lord Manning will be allied with us. Don't you see? No one would dare challenge his men and our elves. The Forestlands will finally be ours."

"And if I refuse?" The question hung heavy between them.

Cyrek softened his voice. "I like to think of myself as a fair man. I offer you a choice." Cyrek placed a hand on each of Lia's shoulders. "You can marry Lord Manning," he paused. "Or, you can watch while these two boys have their heads removed."

Jacob could no longer hold his anger. Spear or no spear, he shouted, "No, Lia. Don't do it!"

The guard swung the flat side of his spear. It connected with a thud to the side of Jacob's head. Colors flashed before Jacob's eyes. Then there was only darkness.

~

When Jacob woke, he knew he was no longer in the castle. It was dusk. There was wet grass beneath his legs. Tree bark cut into his back. He and Orson were tied to a huge oak somewhere deep in the Forestlands.

Jacob struggled and stretched. He kicked. He bit at his ropes. "We have to go back."

Orson simply sat still. "In case you haven't noticed, we have no weapons, no food and no water. And we have no idea where we are." Then Orson took a deep breath. "Did I mention that we're also tied to a tree?"

Jacob glared at him. "They can't make Lia marry Lord Manning. It's my fault she came back to the Forestlands in the first place."

"We didn't have much choice at the time."

"It's still my fault. Even if you won't go, I've got to go back and help her." Jacob tried to pull his hands from their bindings, but it was no use.

"Even if we could get back," Orson told him, "it wouldn't do any good. They've already taken her away."

"What? Where?"

"I saw it just before they put the sack on my head," Orson replied. "They were putting Lia on a fine horse. There were two dozen guards at least. My hunch is that she's already at Lord Manning's castle."

Jacob swore. All this was too much. He hung his head and felt as if he had no power and no hope. What were they going to do now?

And why had Lia said nothing about who she was?

Jacob sat with his eyes closed. Then he heard wings flapping overhead. Jacob's head snapped up. There was the first answer. Jacob cleared all other thoughts from his mind. *Cousin*, he thought.

The answer was sweet. *Yes, Dragon Speaker.* A small butcherbird flew to a low branch. A newborn sparrow hung from his beak. He impaled it on a twig, then flew closer.

Help me with these ropes, Jacob said.

The bird pecked and clawed. In a few minutes, the ropes around Jacob's wrists snapped. Jacob turned to thank him, but the butcherbird had already moved on to his prey.

Jacob thought, *Show me the way through the forest. To the standing stones.* Jacob could find his way from there.

Go northeast one day. Follow to where the sun rises the next. Listen for crow cousins feasting on the dead.

Jacob picked up his bow and arrow, then heard the voice of his friend.

"Hey, what about me?" Orson shouted.

"I thought you were ready to give up," Jacob replied.

"Only when they cut off my arms and legs," Orson told him.

"I thought you might look a bit better without that ugly head of yours," Jacob joked. "But I guess you can come along."

CHAPTER SIX | Draco's Fire

Both Jacob and Orson knew they had no hope of storming Lord Manning's castle. They needed a map, they needed a plan, and they needed some help. They had no choice but to go back to the clearing. Perhaps Aldous could help them. Perhaps he could show them some way to rescue Lia.

When they were still many minutes from the small clearing, Jacob felt the first stirrings of the dragon. He reached out with his mind. What came back knocked Jacob flat on his backside. It wasn't the throaty bellow he had expected.

It was a roar.

Jacob forgot the biting ache in his leg. He ignored the gutted pain of his empty stomach. He ran.

At the crest of a hill, Jacob stopped. *Draco?* Gone was the small helpless baby dragon. In its place stood a towering young dragon.

JACOB! The voice boomed in his head.

Draco was easily forty hands tall — five times the size of a horse. His silver scales shone in the sun. Draco leaned back his square flat head and let out a deafening roar. *JACOB IS BACK!* His huge wings spread wide. The ground shook as Draco raced across the field.

Jacob's joy at seeing Draco turned to panic. *Slow down*, he sent.

Despite his size, Draco was no more than a pup. He knocked Jacob to the ground. His giant tongue drooled across Jacob's face. Jacob felt like he was being slapped with a cow's liver. Draco stomped and jumped. Jacob's teeth shook from the impact.

Draco, stop! Jacob ordered.

Jacob? Draco's ears pulled back against his skull. He lowered his head. He sat and hunched his shoulders like a giant scolded puppy.

Jacob couldn't help it — he laughed. *Oh, Draco. I've missed you.* Jacob wrapped his arms around the dragon's

neck. He was rewarded with another slurp of Draco's tongue.

Aldous hurried toward them. "Thank goodness you're back." The old man's left arm was in a sling. There was a large purple bruise on the side of his face.

"Aldous, what happened?" Orson asked. He avoided Draco's thrashing tail as he walked.

"Have you been fighting?" Jacob patted Draco's head.

"Fighting? Only that blasted beast of yours," Aldous cursed. "Our Draco's grown so fast he's tripping over his own feet. These old bones of mine aren't always fast enough to get out of his way."

Draco. You did this to Aldous?

Draco lowered his head. *Maybe.*

For shame, Draco. Aldous is my good friend. He's your friend.

Draco snorted and bumped his nose against Aldous's hand. *It was an accident. Tell him I didn't mean it.*

Jacob watched Aldous run his wrinkled hand over the dragon's nose. The old man put his arms around Draco's huge neck and hugged him.

I do believe that he already knows that.

Draco shook his head and snorted again. *Good.*

A large rat ran into the clearing. Draco spied it and

roared. In two strides, he had the rat in his mouth. One chomp and it was gone.

Hungry. Draco roared once more. Then he stomped through the long grass in search of another treat.

Hungry. The word made Jacob's stomach growl. He and Orson had found some berries and roots in the woods and a small stream to drink from. But that was all. Jacob ached for rabbit and a warm fire to cook it on.

So Draco hunted and Orson cooked. Later, when the meat of three rabbits sat on the table, the three of them could talk. Aldous told Jacob about the work he'd been doing with Draco. Jacob explained what had happened to Lia. When the stories were finished, it was late at night. Orson went out into the field. In the light of the full moon, he practiced. Thrust. Slice. Withdraw. His sword shone in the moon's glow.

In the shadows, Draco snored and huffed in his sleep.

Aldous tipped back his flask of wine. He belched loudly.

"One thing troubles me," Jacob said. He pulled the wine flask from the old man's hand. He needed Aldous sober to get some answers.

"What is it you wish to know?"

"How did Draco grow so fast? We've been gone less than a month."

"Ah, that." Aldous pointed to the stars. "When it calls to him, the beast must answer."

"I don't understand," Jacob said.

"It's an old story." Aldous reached for the flask that Jacob held. "My memory fades."

Jacob gave Aldous back his wine.

The old man sipped and closed his eyes. "It was on the First Point of Aires — the day when winter ends and spring begins. I was a boy of twelve when I saw Draco's Fire."

"What is Draco's Fire?"

"A comet, boy. Most men see it only once in their lifetime. I pray each night that I live long enough to see it again. Do you know nothing of the prophecy?"

Jacob shook his head. "Only the bits and pieces I've heard. I know it says a dragon will bring the end to the darkness in our land. What does a comet have to do with that?"

"The comet is the prophecy!" Aldous exclaimed. "Seventy-eight years ago it came. Blazed across the night. Like the dragon's own breath, it cut across the stars of Draco. Don't you see, boy? That's when all the troubles began. The darkness. The rule of Manning's family."

Jacob didn't understand and told him so.

Aldous struck his staff against the ground. "The

comet sent us a gift. A magic stone that fell like fire to the earth. A dragon stone." Aldous bowed his head. "But we were selfish back then. Men were full of greed. A battle raged between Lord Manning's father and the villagers. The dragon stone broke into two. The two halves became as different as day and night. One comet stone holds the bright light — the goodness in all of us. The other comet stone holds the darkness."

Jacob leaned in closer. "Where are they now?"

"No one knows where the dark side went." The flames made shadows dance across the old man's face. "Manning holds the other. I fear he's used its power over the Elven lord to win our poor Lia."

"What does this have to do with her?" Jacob asked.

"Don't you see? It's all connected. You. Lia. Our young dragon. The comet. It's coming back to fulfill the prophecy. Our Draco feels it. He grows because he must. To be ready when the comet returns."

"What should I do?" Jacob grabbed the old man by his shoulders.

"Take back the stone from Manning, then seek out the dark stone."

Jacob stopped listening. He was ready to run to his horse and go charging off.

"But not yet, you fool. You're not ready yet." Then

Aldous pointed to the sleeping dragon. "*He's* not ready."

"I have to help Lia." Jacob was frantic. "I have to fulfill the prophecy."

"Yes, you do." Aldous nodded. "But not before you know the rest of what you must do. Not before you've proven yourself."

"I don't understand."

Aldous motioned for Jacob to sit. The old man folded his hands and recited:

> "*When a dragon born of Draco's fire*
> *once more shall walk this earth,*
> *the Chosen One must pay the cost*
> *to test a hero's worth.*"

"The stone only answers to a hero who has proven his worth," Aldous explained. "You have courage, boy. But you haven't proven anything yet."

"Then how do I do it?" Jacob was itching to get going.

"I wish I knew." Aldous spread his hands wide. "That is something only *you* will know … when the time comes."

"Wait, I thought you said that Lord Manning used the stone's powers. How can that be? Manning is no hero."

"That is true. But Manning wasn't always the man he is now." Aldous shook his tired head. "He proved his worth at great cost to us all. But that is an old story, one best left to another day."

Jacob's head ached from all he'd learned. "But I have to do something."

Aldous tipped back the rest of his wine. "You want something to do? Practice with your bow," he urged. "Make a plan. Work with me to help our Draco become the dragon he is meant to be. Then, when you're ready, seize the moment."

CHAPTER SEVEN | **Flying the Dragon**

The weeks that followed were a blur in Jacob's mind. Six hours each day, he and Orson practiced with their weapons. Six hours more, Jacob and Aldous worked with Draco. Jacob ate when he had to. He slept when his body could do no more. Jacob's dreams were always the same. Lia would sit trapped in Lord Manning's castle wondering why he hadn't come to save her. Jacob would be frozen, unable to move. Then he'd wake up in a panic.

At first, Jacob's shoulders ached from drawing his bow. His fingers bled from fitting arrows into quivers.

There were red welts around his leg, but the leather brace let him walk with less of a limp. Soon he could run without tripping.

Each morning, Aldous would bind Jacob's leg again. Each time, it was a new mix of leather and ointment. "With some luck, we can build some strength into this leg of yours."

Jacob could only sigh. A strong left leg would be a miracle.

Orson tried to help Jacob learn to use a sword.

"No, not like that. You're not chopping wood, Jacob."

"I'm never going to be as good as you are with a sword," Jacob complained. "Maybe I should just stick to my bow."

Orson planted his hands on his hips. "Jacob, you handle a bow and arrow better than any man I know. But when a battle gets nasty, you have to get up close to the enemy. A bow's no good for that. You need a sword." Orson danced and thrust with his blade to make his point.

Jacob thumped his fist against his bad leg. "It's no use, Orson. I'll never be able to do that."

Orson wouldn't give up. "We'll just work on your upper thrust. That's the best way to gut an enemy. And you have to learn how to counter another man's blade.

When we get to the castle, the odds will be against us. You'll need your bow *and* a sword."

Jacob saw that his friend wasn't going to back down. He picked up his new sword and practiced through the rest of the day.

One day stretched into another. While Jacob practiced with his weapons, Aldous helped to train Draco. Draco's body grew faster than his ability to control it. Aldous set up games that taught Draco how to run without falling over his own feet. He taught him how to change course without crashing into the hillside. Aldous could never speak to Draco the way Jacob could, but the old man and the dragon were still great friends.

Each night, Jacob stared into their small fire and worried. Was Lia all right? Would she forgive him for not coming to get her right away? Did she want him to come at all?

Draco continued to grow. His scales shone like gem stones. But they were harder than steel. Spikes, like gleaming daggers formed down his neck and tail. Draco's meals changed from rats to deer and cattle.

They'd been in the clearing for fifteen days now. The sun had already set when Jacob stood with Draco on the crest of a cliff. *It's time to take a leap of faith, my friend,* Jacob sent to the dragon.

Jacob patted the jagged scales around the dragon's nose. He stepped back as Draco opened his huge wings. A great gust of wind rocked Jacob on his heels and Draco leapt from the cliff.

I'm flying, Draco thought, his joy surging into Jacob's mind.

Draco dipped and twirled. Like one of Jacob's arrows, he shot straight up into the sky. Then he came sailing down through the clouds. Draco could fly very well, only coming down to land was a problem. But after two or three crash landings, Draco figured it out.

Jacob watched Draco's flying get better each day. Aldous worked hard on making a saddle that was big enough to fit the dragon, but small enough to hold Jacob.

At sunset on the twentieth day, Aldous announced, "I'd say our flying dragon is ready." He handed Jacob the saddle. "How about you, boy? Are you ready?"

Jacob wasn't sure, but there was no real choice. He strapped the saddle to Draco's back. Aldous rigged the harness so that he could tie his legs to the saddle. Jacob wound the reins around his right hand. His heart beat in his throat.

Are you afraid? Draco turned his head to look at his rider.

Yes, Draco, I'm afraid. So let's get going before I change my mind.

The plunge from the cliff almost made Jacob lose his breakfast. Still, he held fast to the harness. Draco dipped and soared. He dove like a hawk toward the earth. For a moment, Jacob thought he would fall off. His knuckles were white from gripping the reins too tight. *Slow down!* he begged.

I'm flying with Jacob! Draco shot up past the clouds.

Jacob caught his breath. The night sky was dotted with stars. The full moon looked so close he could see its face. But it was cold up there. He urged Draco to fly lower.

It was on the twenty-fifth day that Draco scorched a nearby field. It started out as a sneeze. Draco huffed and twitched. *ACHOO!* A ball of fire flew from each nostril. The dry autumn grass burned quickly. It took Aldous and Orson over an hour to put out the fire.

Draco was now fifty hands tall. Hiding him away from the world became harder each day. Draco itched to fly farther each time he took to the sky. His appetite grew as he raided farmers' fields each night. Sheep and goats were added to his favorite things to eat. Sometimes, Jacob wasn't happy with Draco's meals.

Draco, where did you get that? Jacob scolded.

The legs of a ram disappeared down Draco's throat. *I was hungry. I went hunting.* He coughed and spit out its horns.

How are we going to keep you secret if you keep stealing from farmers? Jacob wagged his finger at Draco. *There are more important things to think about than your stomach.*

Draco snorted. He leapt into the air and opened his wings wide.

Draco. You come back here!

Try and make me. Draco's laughter echoed in Jacob's head. Whump! A burning pile of dragon dung landed next to Jacob.

Ugh, Draco! Jacob covered his nose with his hand.

This was the worst part of having a dragon. Draco's mouth wasn't the only thing that shot out fire. Once or twice a day, Draco would leave Jacob a gift. The piles of dung were almost as tall as Jacob. A farmer's cow pasture smelled like a garden compared to this stench. In a few hours, the fire in the dung would burn the pile into a heap of ash. It was smelly ash that Jacob and Aldous would spread out of sight. They knew that footprints weren't the only thing used to track an animal.

Three days later, Jacob sat again in Draco's saddle. He was getting used to the feel of the dragon under him. At least he could keep down his breakfast on the dives and turns. Jacob practiced guiding Draco with the reigns. Then he used thought commands. *Turn left. Go right. Stop.* Jacob repeated the commands until Draco knew what he wanted almost before he thought it.

Jacob and Draco were closing in on a farmer's field when Jacob pulled back on the dragon's reins. Jacob could see the sun peeking over the horizon. They'd been out longer than he realized. *Stop, Draco. It's time to go back to camp.*

Draco shook his head so hard that Jacob almost lost his grip. *I'm hungry. Let's hunt.*

Jacob tried to argue. But it was no use. Draco dipped toward a herd of sheep grazing in the cool morning air. He was almost at tree level when his ears twitched forward.

What is it, Draco? What do you hear? Jacob asked.

Horses. Men are coming.

Draco started a steep climb upwards, but it was too late.

Far below them, men were shouting. "Dragon! It's a dragon!"

Two of Lord Manning's soldiers sat pointing at Jacob and Draco. Their horses pawed the ground in fear.

Jacob panicked. What should they do? If Lord Manning discovered Draco now, all their hopes would be lost.

The soldiers drew their bows. "Kill the dragon," one shouted. Arrows whizzed through the air. One bounced off of Draco's cheek.

The dragon's ears drew back. His nostrils flared. *Hold on, Jacob*, Draco sent. Then he dove to the earth.

The soldiers cried out in fear. They whipped their horses hard and galloped away. But horses were no match for a dragon. In seconds, Draco scooped up the two men in his claws. He brought them kicking and screaming to eye level.

One of the soldiers pulled a knife from his belt. He dug it deep into the fleshy part of Draco's paw. Draco howled. In shock and pain, he let go a fiery ball of dung.

The soldier struck at Draco's paw again, and this time Draco let go. The soldiers were free, free to fall to the ground. The men flailed with their hands and feet as they fell. Then they landed in the flaming mound of dragon dung. Within seconds, their bodies turned to ash.

"Ugh!" Jacob gulped. "When my time comes, let me die some other way."

When Jacob ordered Draco back to camp this time, he obeyed.

After that, Jacob took even greater care. They couldn't risk discovery, not yet. Draco flew only if clouds covered the moon and stars.

During the day, Aldous set up targets on posts in the clearing. He used them to teach Draco to use his tail as a weapon. THUMP. Draco knocked each post down. His tail was as much a weapon as … his dung!

Of course, Orson continued his own workouts. Jacob felt a surge of pride when he watched his friend. He'd never seen anyone handle a sword the way that Orson could. In a better world, he deserved to be a knight.

Jacob wondered what Lia would think of all this. He pictured her face in his mind. He thought about her laugh, her musical voice. He even missed her moody silence.

On the morning of the thirty-first day, a large raven landed on Jacob's shoulder. It brought word from the village. *Lord Manning is taking a bride, the daughter of the Elven lord. He will present his bride-to-be at the Samain Festival.*

"Aldous, Orson, come quickly." Jacob told them the news.

"Good," replied Orson. "It's time we got going. I'm getting restless with no one to fight but the bushes."

"Not so fast, my lads." Aldous folded his arms. He tucked his hands inside the sleeves of his cloak. "Let's think this through first."

Long into the night, the three talked and prepared.

Aldous gave them a map to the castle. Even better, he gave them a map of the castle itself — the hidden halls and secret storerooms. They'd need all their cunning and all their skill to rescue Lia.

Before the sun rose the next morning, Jacob and Orson packed up their weapons and supplies. They said little until Orson asked the big question. "Do you think this could be another trap?"

"Maybe," Jacob replied.

"Remember what happened last time?"

"Yes, but this time we have a plan," Jacob replied. "This time we're ready."

Orson tested the edge of his sword. He just prayed that Jacob was right.

CHAPTER EIGHT | The Samain Festival

Orson scratched at the beard and mustache on his face. Aldous had made it from horse hairs. He glued it to Orson's face with tree sap.

"Stop scratching," Aldous told him. The old man pulled a skull cap tightly over Orson's black hair.

"Your own father wouldn't know you now," Jacob told him. He tied a breast plate around Orson's chest. Then he draped a long brown cloak over Orson's body.

The night before, they'd reviewed their plan many times. Each of them had to know their part to have any hope of success.

Orson was to enter the sword contest, win it, and get invited to the feast. Once inside Lord Manning's castle, he'd find the south door and unlock it. While Aldous distracted the guards, Jacob would sneak inside. Together, Jacob and Orson would take the stone and find Lia. Then, somehow, they'd all get out of there. They planned to meet in Mound Meadow, a safe distance from the castle.

"Let's get going." Orson slapped Jacob's back. "I've got a contest to win."

"You make it sound so simple," Jacob said. He smiled at his good friend.

"Winning the contest will be simple." Orson grinned. "No bragging. Just fact. Getting you into the castle may be tough, but I think we can do it." Orson scratched his beard again. "Getting out with Lia. Now that's the hard part. How are we going to do that?"

"Trust the prophecy," Jacob said. He pushed Orson out of their tent and into the chilly morning.

It was a day's walk to the castle, then an overnight camp before they could enter. Even from afar, the smells of pigs roasting and horse dung mixed in the air. Flutes played nearby. People hurried past. The Samain Festival had begun.

Jacob pulled the hood of his cloak over his head. He

kept his head down and stepped out after Orson. Aldous had bound his leg again. It pinched, but he walked with less of a limp. They couldn't afford to have anyone recognize Jacob.

Jacob, where are you? Jacob what's happening? echoed in Jacob's brain.

They'd left Draco in a cave a few miles south. It had taken all of Jacob's powers to convince Draco to stay. Their plan depended on secrecy and surprise. But Draco was too big to hide and too hard to control. He had to stay where he was.

Still Jacob could feel Draco's unrest. *Stay there!* he ordered.

But, Jacob....

The hurt in Draco's answer made Jacob's heart ache. He softened his thoughts but stayed firm. *Please, my friend. I need you to stay put.*

Jacob followed Orson to the field where the contests would take place. There was rope along one end where people could stand and watch. At the other, a rough stage was set up. Two guards stood rigid with spears in hand. Lord Manning's flag flapped in the wind.

Sitting on the stage was Lord Manning. And next to him sat Lia.

Jacob gulped.

Lia's white gown shimmered in the sun. She wore a crown of white lilies on her head.

Jacob's fists clenched. He was still angry with Lia for lying to him about who she was. And now this — dressed like Lord Manning's bride even before the wedding.

Lord Manning leaned over to ask Lia a question. She nodded stiffly. Manning raised his jeweled hand and stroked her cheek. Then he touched her arm, her hand, her knee.

Why didn't she do something? Jacob wondered. He had seen Lia in battle. She'd taken down men twice Manning's size. Why didn't she stop him now?

Jacob glared at Lia and set his jaw. He'd get Lia out of here, then make her answer his questions.

Jacob moved a little closer. He saw something glint from the opening in Lord Manning's coat. A shiny stone hung from Manning's neck. Jacob caught his breath. It must be the comet stone!

A horn sounded. The contests were beginning.

Orson moved out onto the field to face his first rival. Orson huffed and danced. His sword clanked. In minutes, he had his rival on the ground. And that was just his first victory. He fought many young men through the day. By late afternoon, Orson had his final rival on

the ground, his sword at his throat. When Orson stood up, he smiled at the crowd and to himself. The first part of their plan had worked.

"We have a winner!" the judge called out. He raised Orson's hand high in the air. People shouted and cheered. Orson was presented to Lord Manning as the new champion.

Jacob felt a moment of pride for his friend. He caught Orson's eye. Orson nodded ever so slightly. Then the guards slapped Orson on the back and laughed. The men soon led him inside the castle to celebrate.

An hour later, Jacob met Aldous near the north gate of the castle.

Aldous grinned widely when he heard of Orson's win. "Now to make some noise," he said. "Any time you're ready."

Jacob cleared his mind. He searched the trees and called to the fields. *Cousins, come to me!* Birds of every shape and colour filled the air. Hawks flew with sparrows. Doves soared with crows. *Help this good man keep the guards busy,* he told them, nodding at Aldous.

"I can handle this from here." Aldous patted Jacob's shoulder. "Be off. And good luck."

Jacob ducked into the shadows. He crept south along the castle wall. Inside he could hear guards shouting and running. Behind him, birds cawed and shrieked. No one noticed Jacob sneak to the southern door.

Jacob tried the door latch. It clicked open. "Thank you," he whispered to Orson. The second part of their plan had worked.

Orson nodded to his friend, then went back to the victory party.

As quietly as he could, Jacob moved through the halls. Torches burned along the walls so his shadow stretched across the floor. Jacob followed his nose more than Aldous's map. He could smell roasted ox, potatoes and cabbage. He was getting closer to the great chamber. That was where Lord Manning dined with his knights. That's where Lia would be.

The hall got wider just ahead. Jacob heard laughter and the clink of cups. He stayed close to the wall, in the shadows. There were six huge wooden braces at the entrance to the chamber. When no one was looking, Jacob climbed one. Oak beams crossed the ceiling. The beams held the giant wheel of candles that lit the room. Carefully, Jacob climbed onto a ceiling beam. He inched his way to the center of the room.

Below him, Jacob could see Lia at the head of the table with Lord Manning. The wizard Kain sat apart from the group. Kain tossed meat to Manning's hounds and watched them fight over it.

Orson was seated with all the knights. Their voices floated up to Jacob.

"Friends, I have a question." Orson spoke to the knights who sat next to him. One had a nasty black eye. The other's arm was in a sling. "What battle gave you those hurts?"

The knights roared with laughter.

Lord Manning raised a hand to silence them. He'd already had too much wine. His voice was slurred. "It seems my Lia has a strong spirit," Lord Manning said. He winked at his men. "But not to worry. We've taken care of that. Haven't we, darling?" Manning put one hand on Lia's shoulder. The other rubbed the shining that stone hung around his neck.

Lia stared at her plate of uneaten food.

Jacob looked at the top of Lia's bowed head. He saw how her hands were clenched tightly into fists. Jacob's heart softened. He willed her to look at him. *Lia. Look up.*

Slowly Lia raised her head. Her eyes widened when she saw him. Then she smiled.

The third part of their plan had worked. Now only the hardest part remained. How would they get Lia out of Lord Manning's castle?

CHAPTER NINE | "It Took You Long Enough."

For the first time, Lia dared a quick look at Orson. Orson winked back. Lia turned her gaze back at the table. Only later did she raise her head again. This time there was a question in her eyes.

Jacob pointed to Lord Manning. He pointed to Lia. Then he pointed to the door.

The look on Lia's face said, *Are you crazy?*

Jacob repeated the gestures. First Manning, then Lia, then the door. His face glared back at her. *Do it now!*

Manning raised his wine cup to drink. Lia pulled it from his hand and took a big gulp, then she linked her arm in his. "It's much too crowded in here." Her voice was all honey and sweetness.

"Relax, darling," Lord Manning told her. "Enjoy the party." He poured more wine and spilled as much on the table as in his cup.

"I'd rather enjoy it with you. Just the two of us." Lia lay her head on Manning's shoulder.

Jacob almost fell off the beam. This wasn't what he'd had in mind when he had signaled to Lia.

Manning quickly downed his wine. He slapped his cup back on the table and grinned. "I knew if I gave you enough time, you'd come around." He stood quickly and knocked over his chair.

Arm in arm, he and Lia headed for the door. Manning's personal guards got up to follow.

"Are they coming, too?" Lia giggled.

"Now, darling, you know they always go where I go."

Lia put her arm around Manning's waist. "Even to your chamber?"

That was enough to change Manning's mind. "My good fellows," Manning said to his guards. "Stay. Enjoy the party. My lady and I will be having our own private party."

Jacob's blood boiled. Manning was enjoying this far too much.

The knights stomped their feet and cheered. Manning bowed clumsily to his men. Then he led Lia out the door.

Jacob and Orson used the noise to make their way out of the great hall. They followed the sound of Manning's voice as he and Lia walked to his chamber.

"Our Lia is quite the actress," Orson whispered.

"Shut up and follow them." Jacob could feel the heat burning his face. Part of him knew that this was the only way Lia could get Lord Manning alone. The other part of him wanted to rip Manning's face off.

At the dark end of a long hallway, Jacob and Orson stopped.

Ahead of them, down the hall, were Lord Manning and Lia. Manning had pushed Lia against a large oak door. "This is my bedchamber," Manning whispered. He nibbled the curve of Lia's neck.

Manning wasn't prepared for what Lia did next. As hard as she could, Lia slammed her knee into his groin. Lord Manning crumbled to the floor. Lia's hand was over his mouth before he could call out.

Jacob and Orson rushed forward. They pulled the sash from around Manning's waist and stuffed it in his mouth. Jacob took some rope from his pocket and tied Manning's hands. Then he tied the rope to the handle of the door.

"It took you long enough." Lia glared at Jacob and Orson. "How long were you going to leave me here?"

"From what I saw, you weren't trying very hard to get away," Jacob snapped back.

CRACK! Lia slapped Jacob's face. Hard. "I didn't have any choice. Thanks to the stone he's got around his neck, I've been trapped here."

Jacob ignored his aching cheek. "The comet stone!" He reached into Manning's coat and pulled out the chain. The strange stone swung in his hand. It shone brighter than the torches on the castle walls.

Manning tried to curse through his gag. He squirmed in his bindings. Jacob pressed down with his boot to hold Manning still. Then he lifted the chain off Manning's neck. Gently, Jacob put it around his own neck. It felt cool on his skin.

"How could a stone trap you here?" Jacob asked.

"Could you two talk about this later?" Orson asked. He shuffled from foot to foot, eager to get going.

Lia ignored Orson. "Manning said that the stone would give him whatever he wanted most. But only if he wanted it badly enough."

"And he wanted you." Jacob couldn't stop the redness in his face.

"I'm here, aren't I?" Lia stood with her hands on her hips.

Orson stepped in between them. "If you two don't mind. . . ." he bgan. "If we're going to escape, now would be a very good time."

The sound of a door opening and closing at the end of the hall stopped all debate. Jacob put his finger to his lips and pointed to the hall leading south. Soon they were running down the shadowy hall.

Jacob couldn't relax until the south door came into view. One more hall and they'd be out of the castle and on their way home. They were that close when a crash like thunder split the silence.

The three of them froze. The sound of laughter echoed around their heads. Kain's voice seemed to come from all directions. "You didn't think it was going to be that easy. Did you?"

CHAPTER TEN | Kain's Collection

Jacob drew his bow from under his cloak. He pulled a dagger from his belt and threw it to Lia. Orson drew his sword.

Together they formed a circle in the middle of the hall, their feet spread in battle stance.

Jacob looked to the south door and down the length of the hall. There were many doors that led into the hallway. Kain could be behind any one of them. "Show yourself," Jacob called.

The air filled with Kain's laughter. "Patience, boy. All in good time."

Jacob looked behind them. What to do? It wouldn't be long before the guards found Manning. It was too risky to bolt for one of the rooms. He had no idea what lay behind any of the doors.

Jacob looked again to the south door. Only moments ago it had seemed so near. Now it seemed a lifetime away.

"Got any great ideas?" Orson shifted from foot to foot. His sword was held tight in both hands.

"Stick to the plan." Jacob pointed to the south door. He showed him three fingers.

Orson raised his eyebrows but nodded.

Jacob scanned the hall one last time. He raised his fingers again. One. Two. Three. "Now!" he called.

They raced down the hall toward the south door.

Kain appeared in a puff of smoke. He bared his pointed teeth and growled. "I've been looking forward to this." From his belt he pulled a shimmering whip. It thrashed and twisted like a living snake.

CRACK! Kain gave a warning strike against a solid oak door. The wood sizzled where the whip touched it.

"Do you like my new toy?" the wizard asked.

Jacob let loose an arrow.

Kain swatted it away like a fly. "You know you'll have to do better than that, boy."

Orson charged with his sword, but Kain's whip

knocked it from his hands. The tip of the whip hissed against Orson's breast plate. Sparks spit across the metal.

Then it was Lia's turn. She aimed her blade at Kain's throat and let it fly.

Kain ducked easily out of its way. "Is that the best you can do, little girl?"

Orson picked up his sword and moved close to Jacob. "What now?"

"He can't fight all of us at once," Jacob whispered. He pulled Lia close to him. "Together now!" he shouted.

All three charged Kain. Orson and Lia were on either side of Jacob as they barreled down the hallway.

Kain spun with his whip. It hissed through the air. Then he kicked out with his foot.

Orson and Lia went sprawling.

Jacob used the moment to fall to the floor. He slid beneath Kain's whip, then came up hard. With the heel of his hand, Jacob used all his strength to connect with Kain's chin.

It worked. Kain's head snapped back. His pointed teeth ripped into his upper mouth and Kain cried out in pain. Blood as black as his heart spurted from his mouth.

"Run!" Jacob shouted. The wizard's dark blood dripped down his hair and onto his face.

Orson paused. He and Lia were within reach of the door. "We're not leaving you."

"Don't argue," Jacob ordered. "Get her out of here."

For a moment, Jacob thought Orson wasn't going to listen. He looked to the door and then at Lia, waiting for her to move. Orson raised his fist in a salute. Then he and Lia rushed out the door into the darkness.

Kain recovered quickly. He struck Jacob hard with the butt of his whip. Jacob's bow went flying across the hall. Jacob's leg buckled under him. He sprawled in a heap on the floor.

"Do you think I care about your friends?" Kain breathed heavily. He grabbed Jacob by the collar and dragged him along the floor like a sack of flour. "You're the one I want, boy."

Jacob's weak leg twisted as he was dragged. He cried out as the leather bindings cut into his flesh.

Kain grinned through his bloodied teeth. "You think that hurts? Wait until I'm done with you."

They finally reached a double door at the end of the hall. Carved into the door was the crest of a falcon eating a snake. Kain laughed as he pushed Jacob through it. "Here we are, boy. Home, sweet home."

Jacob's ears rang as he was thrown to the floor. The

air was knocked out of him in one mighty whoosh. It took a moment for his vision to refocus.

The room was huge, with stone walls and a giant domed ceiling. Black curtains flapped in the breeze.

Jacob raised his head and cursed, "You vile piece of. . . ."

They'd entered Kain's spell room. Dozens of dragon's teeth were displayed like trophies on his walls. The smallest was the length of Jacob's arm.

"Do you like my collection?" Kain traced his fingers lovingly along the lines of a huge dragon's tooth. Then he moved to an empty spot in the center of the wall. "I've reserved this place of honour, though, for one special dragon."

Jacob ignored the searing pain in his leg. He leapt to his feet. "No!"

"Did you really think that all this was about you, boy?" Kain threw back his head and laughed. "What use would I have for a boy with a twisted leg? Unless, of course, I can use you as bait." Kain shook his head so that the teeth in his hair rattled like a snake.

"No, I won't let you." Jacob dove at Kain like a wild animal.

Kain raised his fist. He slammed it against the side of Jacob's head and sent him flying backwards. "And how do you plan to stop me?" Kain grabbed Jacob by the throat and smashed him against the wall.

"I'll stop you. . . ." Jacob couldn't get any more words out.

Kain tightened his grip around Jacob's throat.

Jacob couldn't breathe. He couldn't think. The world around Jacob went gray and slowly turned to black.

CHAPTER ELEVEN | No, Draco. Go Back!

A small part of Jacob's brain tried to gain control. His life couldn't end like this. He couldn't let it. But Jacob could feel his arms and legs go slack. His neck could no longer hold up his head. His eyes rolled back. *Fight it!* Jacob told himself. He wanted to punch and kick. But his body wouldn't obey.

Kain's fingers reach into Jacob's mouth. The sharp point of a knife dug into Jacob's gums. Jacob tasted blood as the blade pushed beneath the roots of his teeth. White hot pain shot through Jacob as Kain yanked out the tooth.

Jacob did not have the strength to fight back. If he was going to survive, he needed to draw on something else. He needed the strength of his mind.

Jacob called up the stillness from inside. He commanded his racing heart to slow. He calmed his gasping lungs to save what little air was left in them. Jacob harnessed all the power he knew into staying alive. *Feathers*, he thought. *Think of soft things. Gentle things.*

But what came back to Jacob wasn't soft. It wasn't gentle. It was a roar.

JACOB!

There was a crash like thunder. Wood and bricks went flying. Something had smashed the castle's outside wall.

It was Draco!

Kain shouted, "At last!" He let loose his grip on Jacob's throat and faced the dragon.

Jacob put his hands to his neck. He gulped air into his lungs. *No, Draco. Go back!* Jacob forced the thought through the fog in his brain.

But Draco wasn't listening. Gone was the gentle dragon that Jacob rode through the clouds. In his place stood a snapping, snarling beast. Draco let out an ear-splitting roar. Then a ball of flame shot from his mouth and nostrils.

But Kain was ready for that. A swirling ball of light formed in Kain's hand. When he tossed it high into the air, it swallowed most of the dragon's fire. What remained set Kain's cloak ablaze as he jumped out of its path.

Kain ripped off his cloak. He threw it to the floor and grinned at Draco. "Such a fine young dragon. It's a pity you have to die." Then Kain reached for his whip. "See how much I admire you, dragon." The whip snaked and hissed through the air. "I made this whip just for you."

The whip cracked against Draco's skin. The dragon roared in pain.

Jacob could smell the flesh beneath Draco's scales burning. He tried to get up, but Jacob made it only to his knees.

Kain laughed and snapped his whip again. Draco let out another roar of pain. Draco tried to swipe at Kain with his claws, but Kain dove out of reach.

The dragon was now wild with pain. Balls of flame exploded from him. He lashed with his tail. The floor and walls shook from its blows.

Each time, Kain managed to control the fire and stay out of reach. "Come, dragon. You can do better than that," he taunted.

Jacob tried to shake the cobwebs from his brain. He

gulped more air into his lungs. *Get up!* he told himself. He tried again and crumbled to the floor.

Kain let his whip fly. It caught Draco just below the left eye. Draco howled. He stretched his giant neck to its full height. Then the dragon pulled back his head to let loose more balls of fire.

It was the moment that Kain was waiting for. The whip hissed through the air. It connected with the soft flesh beneath Draco's chin. A gash opened. Blood poured onto the cold stone floor.

Draco shook his head and snorted. Then he crashed in a heap on the floor.

"No!" Jacob cried. He forced himself to his feet. He stumbled and fell. Then he forced himself up again.

Kain raised both fists to the sky and howled. "Victory!" He shook his fist at Jacob. "What a glorious day!"

Jacob was on his knees, trying to figure out what to do.

Kain showed Jacob the bloody tooth in his hand. "One for my hair. And, next, one for my wall."

Kain pulled his blood-soaked dagger from his belt. He headed toward Draco's limp body.

At last, Jacob forced his legs to stand. His knees were like pudding. Blood still dripped from his mouth. His head throbbed. But Jacob focused on putting one foot in front of the other. He limped to the wall, then leaned against it to steady himself. *What can I do?*

Kain grunted as he forced Draco's mouth open. He stroked his fingers across the jagged row of teeth. "Ah, what a perfect prize." His words were almost a prayer. Kain raised his dagger high.

Jacob lifted his spinning head and looked around the room. Jacob had lost his bow in the hall. He had no weapon. He had no strength. How could he stop Kain?

Jacob felt dizzy again. He groped the wall for support. His hand felt the cold ivory of a large dragon's tooth. It shifted as he leaned against it. And Jacob got an idea.

Jacob felt the blood surge through him. He seized the tooth from the wall. Then Jacob charged the crouching wizard.

"Kain!" he shouted.

Kain stood and turned. At first, he simply looked annoyed. Then his eyes widened. The first look was replaced with one of disbelief.

Jacob called on the last of his strength. He pulled the tooth back, then rammed it hard, into Kain's stomach.

Kain gripped his stomach with his hands. Inky blood spilled around his fingers. He coughed and more blood seeped from his mouth.

Jacob was filled with rage as he pulled the dragon's tooth from Kain's stomach. This wizard had killed his family. Now he tried to kill the world's last dragon. It was too much.

Jacob's legs shook beneath him from the strain. His lungs were on fire. His heart knocked against his ribs. He was about to ram the tooth into Kain again when the wizard cried out.

"Stop." Kain raised his bloody hands in defeat. He lowered his head. "You have me, boy." Kain tossed his knife and whip to the floor.

Jacob kicked the weapons out of reach. Still, he kept the tooth raised high.

"I said you have me." Kain's chest rose and fell. It was an effort for him to breathe.

Jacob glared at Kain. He raised the dragon's tooth higher.

Kain searched Jacob's face with his eyes. A cold smile spread across Kain's face. "Do it, boy. Taste the sweet wine of murder."

CHAPTER TWELVE | The Comet Stone

Kain's death. There was nothing Jacob wanted more at that moment. Rage burned through him, hotter than a dragon's breath.

"You killed my family!" Jacob declared. His hands shook. Hate snaked its way into his heart.

"Then strike." Kain opened his arms wide. He leaned back his head and closed his eyes.

Jacob saw the satisfaction in Kain's face just before the wizard closed his eyes. He stopped for a moment and thought about what he was doing. "Strike and become like you?" Jacob lowered the dragon's tooth. "Not like this. No, not like this!"

"I didn't think you had the backbone for it," Kain said, grinning at him. Blood stained his cloak and pooled on the floor.

Off in the distance, a horn blew. Doors opened and slammed shut again. Jacob heard shouts and feet running. He knew the guards were on their way.

Jacob turned his head toward the doors leading to the hallway. It was only for a moment. But it was long enough for Kain.

The wizard reached into the pocket of his robe. He pulled out a small clear orb. Before Jacob could stop him, he smashed it on the floor. "Away with me!" he shouted. Soon smoke circled Kain. It made a pool where he knelt, then coiled around his knees and moved upward. It swirled like a funnel cloud and lifted Kain into the air.

The wizard's voice echoed through the room. "You have won this battle, boy. But the war is far from over!"

Then Kain was gone. The only thing left of him was a black pool of blood on the floor.

Jacob ran to the double doors. He could hear the guards stomping through the halls. The sound got louder with each thump, thump, thump.

Jacob looked for something to brace the doors. The

dragon's tooth in his hand still dripped Kain's black blood. He jammed the tooth through the door handles. "Please, God, let that hold them."

Then Jacob ran to the dragon's side.

Draco! he sent the thought.

There was no answer.

Draco, please wake up. They're coming!

Still, there was nothing.

Jacob put his hand over the dragon's nose. No air came through it. The dragon, the last male fire dragon on earth, was still and silent.

Jacob got closer. He wrapped his arms around Draco's giant neck. Jacob laid his head against the rough scales. The pulse should have been like the pounding of drums. But Draco's pulse was barely a whisper.

Draco? Jacob ran his hand lovingly over the dragon's neck. His fingers came back slick with blood.

"Please," Jacob prayed to everything that he held holy. "I offer you anything you wish. Take my life instead. Just don't let him die."

A dark hole opened up in Jacob's thoughts. The bond between their minds was fading. He could feel life leaving the dragon. Jacob knew he had to do something, but what?

The comet stone still hung round Jacob's neck. It began to glow. Like a beating heart, it started to throb.

Jacob felt a spark enter him. Liquid light seemed to surge through his veins.

The light seeped from his pores. It was as if Jacob and the stone had become one.

Jacob bent down and used all his strength to turn Draco's head. He could see the giant gash on the underside of the dragon's throat.

Jacob removed the chain that held the stone from his neck. *You must live, Draco,* he urged. Then he placed the stone against the tear in Draco's flesh.

Sparks of light, like tiny stars, formed over Draco. In one great burst, they exploded upwards. When they reached the ceiling, the sparks stopped. There they formed the shape of Draco's stars in the night sky. Then the spark dragon dove toward the dying Draco. It swirled and spun around his head. Faster and faster the sparks raced. They skimmed the length of Draco's back. They curved around his tail. When they reached the tip of Draco's tail, the stars exploded. The room was showered with a million slivers of light.

Jacob felt the spark leave him. The stone he pressed against the dragon's wound dimmed. It was cool in his hand.

Draco? Jacob laid his head against the dragon's neck. He could feel a pulse.

Jacob? Draco opened one eye and then the other. He lifted his head weakly.

Jacob watched as the wound in Draco's neck closed. It was truly a miracle — or very strong magic.

In the hall outside, Jacob heard the guards shout. "In here!" they called. The guards pounded on the doors.

Jacob turned to Draco. *Draco, can you move? We have to get out of here.*

The room shook with the sound of axes chopping at the doors. Someone shouted, "Hurry, before they get away!"

Draco, please. I know you're weak. But you've got to try. Jacob stroked Draco's face as he pleaded.

Draco's huge body trembled as he tried to stand. Then he crashed back to the floor. *I can't. It's too hard.*

You must try again. Jacob braced his shoulders under Draco's chin. He dug his heels in and tried to lift. It was useless, like an ant trying to move a mountain. *Please, Draco!*

Draco tried again. Slowly, shakily he got to his feet.

Jacob mounted the dragon's back. He wrapped his arms around one of the spikes that poked from Draco's spine. *Just take us outside the castle.* Jacob focused all his strength into the soothing words he sent. *It's only a little way. You can do it.* Jacob held on tight. He kicked the dragon with his heels. *Now fly!*

Draco opened his wings just as the doors gave in. A dozen guards spilled into the room. Arrows whizzed past Jacob's head. He ducked and held on.

Draco jumped through the broken wall. He leapt into the air. He soared just above the tree line.

When they had flown almost to Mound Meadow, Draco faltered. His huge eyes rolled back into his head. His neck went slack. With a mighty thud, Draco crashed to the earth.

~

Aldous, Orson and Lia were waiting. Jacob was thrown to the ground when Draco crashed, but he wasn't badly hurt.

Soon the sun would set. Jacob prayed for the red globe to hurry its way down past the tree line. In the darkness, they would be safe; in the light of day, they could still be found.

Jacob looked over his shoulder for the hundredth time. "Hurry!" he shouted to Orson and Aldous. "If the guards get here before the sun sets, this is never going to work."

Draco lay breathing heavily. *Are we safe?* It was an effort for him to keep his eyes open. *It hurts.*

Jacob could feel the fear and the pain coming from Draco. The poor dragon was exhausted, but he couldn't rest.

It's all right, my friend, Jacob sent to him. *We're safe for now. You've done your part. Let us do ours.*

Draco sighed deeply and gave in to sleep.

Lia leaned against the sleeping Draco. She ran her hands over his wounds. She rubbed ointment into the flesh between his scales. The ointment smelled like pine needles and rotting leaves. Her body swayed as she chanted healing spells.

Mound Meadow was named well. It was dotted with large grassy mounds. Each was the size of a small hill. If Jacob had his way, the guards would only see another mound when they arrived — not a very large dragon.

"More leaves. More earth!" Jacob called. He dug up the ground with his bare hands.

Orson cut away brush with his sword. "Here, lay this across Draco's flank and tail."

Aldous cut reeds and ferns from a nearby marsh. Jacob climbed Draco's back and Aldous handed bundles of green up to him.

They all worked quickly. By the time the sun was only a fingernail above the hills, they were finished. Draco was covered from nose to tail with earth and greenery. In the failing light, he looked just like one of the grassy mounds.

Orson and Aldous crawled into the gap between Draco's leg and his curled tail. They wrapped their cloaks around their heads and shoulders. Then Jacob covered them with ferns. Lia squeezed into the space next to Draco's cheek. Jacob covered her with brush branches first. Then he crawled in beside her. He pulled a large pine bough over himself.

It was none too soon.

Jacob could hear them — horses, soldiers, hunting dogs.

Jacob peeked through the branches. Torches dotted the fields that flanked the meadow. When Jacob put his hand to the ground, the earth trembled. There must have been twenty horses. They were heading straight toward the spot where Draco lay hidden.

Be still, Draco, Jacob sent. *Sleep*.

There was nothing left now but to wait.

CHAPTER THIRTEEN | Sacrifice

Each minute seemed to stretch on forever. Lord Manning's soldiers were close. Their dogs were barking as they searched for Draco. One movement, one sound and they'd all be caught.

Jacob's leg throbbed from his fall with Draco. His tongue traveled again into the hole where his tooth used to be. His neck muscles ached from straining to peer through the branches. And his heart thudded from being so close to Lia.

"Lia," Jacob whispered. "About what I said to you at the castle."

Lia put her hand over his mouth. The shock was like a tiny bolt of lightning that moved from her fingers to his lips.

"I know," she whispered. "You were crude and stupid. But would you mind apologizing some other time? We're a bit busy right now."

Crude? Stupid? Jacob felt his temper flare. "Who said I was apologizing?"

"Shhh. They're close."

Jacob would have continued, but Lia was right. The sounds of horses drifted across the meadow. The guards were coming closer.

It was tense as the guards searched around them. One guard came so close that Jacob could see his horse's breath in the cold night air. One dog seemed to sniff at Draco's tail, but could not tell the leafy mound was a sleeping dragon.

Jacob shivered again. It was awfully cold without a fire to stay warm. Jacob brushed against Lia. Her skin was like ice. She was drained from the healing spell she'd done for Draco. Her Elven blood was no longer able to fight the cold.

Jacob felt his anger fade. He put his arm around Lia and pulled her close. The least he could do was keep her warm.

At first, Lia's whole body tensed. Jacob rubbed her shoulders to let her know that his only aim was to warm her. She stayed stiff for a moment. Then, with her teeth chattering, Lia leaned her head on his chest. Jacob closed his eyes and let his body warm hers.

It was a full hour before the guards gave up their search of Mound Meadow. Jacob could hear one of the guards complain, "The Captain's out of his mind. Searching this soggy meadow, argh. Where does he think they're hiding that monster of a dragon? Under a tree leaf?"

Jacob, Lia and the others remained under their cover of green until just before dawn. Lia never really slept. She continued her healing spell with Draco. An hour before sunrise, she sighed. "That's the best I can do for now. He's strong enough to be moved, but no more than that. We have to get Draco somewhere safe where I can work with him some more."

Jacob pulled a pine branch away and left their hiding spot. He stretched in the darkness. Then he woke Orson and Aldous.

"I need to get Draco away before sunrise," he told them. "I'm going to try to get him to fly to the clearing. Then you can follow on foot."

"And if he can't do the flight?" Orson asked. How could they ever move a fully grown dragon?

Jacob had no answer. He turned his thoughts to the sleeping dragon. *Draco*, he sent, *wake, my friend. Just one more flight. To our old campsite.*

Draco's thoughts were sleepy. *I ache all over. I'm tired.*

Jacob could feel the strain in Draco's answer. *I know, my brave dragon. Just one more time. Then you can rest.*

Draco shook the remaining leaves from his back. He leaned down for Jacob to mount his back. Then he spread his wings and soared into the air.

~

The moon was already in the sky when Orson, Aldous and Lia joined Jacob at their old campsite. The events of the last few days had caught up with Jacob. His body and mind were drained. He'd slept most of the day while Draco rested.

Orson started a small fire to ward off the growing cold. Even that was risky. As far as any of them knew, their hiding place was still secret. But how long would that last? No place would be safe for long.

Orson grinned at Jacob in the moonlight. "Thought you might be hungry." He dropped a string of dead rabbits next to the fire. Together, they gutted the rabbits and cooked them. An hour later, Jacob's belly was full for the first time in days. He looked up as Lia came to sit beside him.

"I hope you saved me some of that rabbit."

Jacob handed her a bit of meat. "How is Draco?"

Lia dug into the food. "Better," she said between bites. "I've done all I can for now. I think he'll be ready to fly a little by morning."

Jacob's heart ached when he looked at her. There were dark circles under her green eyes. Her skin was almost white. Her head drooped. Her hands shook.

"You should rest now, Lia," Jacob told her.

"I'll be fine, just give me a moment. . . ." She never finished her sentence.

"Lia?"

Then Jacob heard a soft snore. Lia had fallen asleep sitting up.

Jacob grinned and shook his head. Orson went to where she still sat up and gently laid her down. Then he put his cloak over her. He nodded to Jacob, then went off to keep watch through the night.

Jacob couldn't sleep. He sat and watched the flames dance in the dark.

When Aldous returned, the old man pulled out his drinking flask. "Something to warm your bones?"

Jacob shook his head and kept staring into the fire. "I

wonder if I'll ever be warm again, Aldous. I wonder if we'll ever get out of this alive."

Aldous tipped back his wine, then patted Jacob's shoulder. "It's true. You've paid a high price these past months. But you rescued the last male fire dragon. You've proven your worth as a hero. And you fulfilled the first part of the prophecy."

"The first part?" Jacob asked. "You mean there's more?"

Aldous took a long drink of his wine. "One length of the road is traveled, boy. But your journey is not over."

"What do you mean?"

Aldous leaned in close. "The prophecy has more to reveal to you. You hold a piece of it around you neck." He pointed to the comet stone. "In time, the stone will lead you to the next leg of your journey. Great deeds require great sacrifice."

"Sacrifice? Haven't I sacrificed enough?" Jacob shot back. "I lost my family. I almost lost Draco. I've almost been killed myself. What more can the prophecy ask of me?"

"More." Aldous sighed and spread his hands wide. "It will ask for much more before it is done, my son. I know that is not what you want to hear. But it is the way of the prophecy, all the same."

"Why didn't you tell me this sooner?" Jacob felt his heart sinking.

"Would you have had the courage to come this far if I had?"

A good question, Jacob thought. Would any hero risk this much if he knew what it would cost? Jacob had no family, no village, no life beyond the prophecy. He felt trapped in his own destiny.

Aldous suddenly looked every one of his ninety years. "No more questions, young man. The future will come soon enough." Aldous turned his back to Jacob and laid down. Within minutes, he was asleep.

Jacob sat and stared into the fire for hours. He was bone weary, but sleep would not come. His mind was too full of what Aldous had told him.

The sun was peeking over the tree line when Orson returned from his watch. Jacob woke the others. Silently, the foursome broke camp. They'd have to find a new hiding place, and then another one after that. Sooner or later, Lord Manning would find them. And what would they do then?

Jacob watched Orson tie a pack of supplies onto Draco's saddle. His usually cheerful face was dark and pensive. "What's wrong?"

Orson sighed. "When we first started this, I thought

we were going to have a great adventure." Orson tightened the pack. "But being a hero isn't what I thought it would be. We do more hiding than fighting. And we still don't know how all this will end."

Jacob forced a smile for Orson's sake. "If you knew what was going to happen, would you have started all this?" It was the question that Aldous had asked. And still there was no answer.

Jacob mounted Draco's saddle. The others got ready for a long day's march.

Jacob snapped the reins. *Away, Draco,* he sent. The great dragon spread his wings and together they soared into the clouds. Together they flew into an unknown future.

The Prophecy

When night skies blaze with Draco's fire
the darkest days shall come
until the Chosen One will rise
to speak in bird and dragon tongue.

When a dragon born of Draco's fire
once more shall walk this earth,
the Chosen One must pay the cost
to test a hero's worth.

Two become one, or one shall fail:
The Chosen One's birthright.
That which was broken must be healed,
When fire burns the night.

THE LAST DRAGON
by **C.A. Rainfield**

*Book One of the
Dragon Speaker Series*

In the year 1144, dark times have fallen over the kingdom. Lord Manning rules through fear and magic, and the only hope seems to lie in the prophecy.

The prophecy says that a Dragon Speaker will appear to save the kingdom. Yet there are no dragons and no one who knows how to speak to them ... except, perhaps, Jacob of Malden. Jacob is an unlikely hero – a small young man who walks with a limp and has the power to speak with birds.

But when the last dragon returns, it is only Jacob who can speak with her. It is only Jacob who can call upon her help. And ultimately it is Jacob – with his friends Orson and Lia – who rescues the egg holding the world's last male dragon.

ISBN 978-1-897039-46-5
www.hip-books.com/fantasy
A teacher's guide is available to cover all three novels.

DRACO'S FIRE
by **E.L. Thomas**

Book Three of the
Dragon Speaker Series

To fulfill the prophecy, Jacob must bring together the two parts of the comet stone. Jacob expects his friend Orson to help, but Orson betrays him. Soon Lord Manning has both Orson and Lia under his control. He's ready to force Lia into marriage.

Jacob has only his own courage, and Draco the fully grown dragon, on his side. But the comet returns, and magic can sometimes work miracles. Draco's fire is only one part of a spectacular finish to the Dragon Speaker trilogy.

ISBN 978-1-897039-48-9

www.hip-books.com/fantasy

A teacher's guide is available to cover all three novels.

About the Author

D.M. Ouellet is an accomplished author of poetry and children's stories but has always loved fantasy. Her recent children's book, *How Robin Saved the Spring* (illustrated by Nicoletta Ceccoli), has received enthusiastic reviews across North America. Visit her website at www.debbieouellet.com for more information about all of her writing.

For more information on HIP novels:
High Interest Publishing
www.hip-books.com
391 Wellesley St. E. Toronto, Ontario M4X 1H5
2495 Main St. #452 Buffalo, New York 14214